YAWWNNNNNN!

Love you!
Bye, Mama!

Have fun, Freddy!

MY TEACHER IS A ROBOT

 Published in the United States by Crown Books for Young Readers, an imprint of Random House Children's Books, a division of Penguin Random House LLC, New York.

Crown and the colophon are registered trademarks of Penguin Random House LLC.

Visit us on the Web! rhcbooks.com

Educators and librarians, for a variety of teaching tools, visit us at RHTeachersLibrarians.com

Library of Congress Cataloging-in-Publication Data is available upon request.

ISBN 978-0-553-53451-1 (trade)
ISBN 978-0-553-53452-8 (lib. bdg.)
ISBN 978-0-553-53453-5 (ebook)

10 9 8 7 6 5 4 3 2 1

MANUFACTURED IN CHINA

First Edition

Random House Children's Books supports the First Amendment and celebrates the right to read.

Did you hear me, Fred? How are we starting the day?
Alejandra
Miriam
Derek
Edgar
Latasha

Uh, math?
Good listening! Take out your workbooks and turn to page 11...
It was a lucky guess. Robots love math.
1/725
11 94
38 327
2187
23
421

Fred, what are you doing? We're supposed to finish story problem #38.
Don't you see that, Annabelle?
See what?

SPIDER!
Cool!
Why is everyone bugging out?

I like spiders. They eat the other bugs.
Actually, spiders are arachnids, not insects.

Was that even a spider? I only count six legs.
There's the other two, Derek.
You kids have too much energy!
smoosh

Grab your jackets and head out to recess. No running!
Who is your hero?
Isn't running the whole point of recess?
I thought Mr. Bailey would like how excited we were during math.
He wants us to be boring robots, just like him!

Guys, do you feel raindrops?
I don't. I'm outrunning them!
Mud monsters are coming!

Super team, engage!
Kids, come back inside!
What are you trying to do, Miriam?
Control the weather with my mind! It's not working.

It's time for history now, anyway.
Why is Mr. Bailey scared of a little rain?
Getting wet will short out his circuitry!

History? Like... like DINOSAURS?

ROARR
Maybe today won't be boring after all!

RRRRRR!
I read that dinosaurs didn't actually roar.
That's right, Edgar. Also, dinosaurs are PRE-history. We're studying HISTORY—of Japan.
ANCIENT JAPAN

Did you know they ate sushi during the Edo period, Alvin?
You can do your research with a partner.
Who wants to sumo wrestle?

Hold that pose, Alejandra.
Fred, make some samurai armor with us!
Shhhh!
That looks more like a ROBOT suit.

RINNGGGGGGG!
Can't you see Mr. Bailey is turning you into robots?!
You're all probably getting hungry. Let's clean up this mess and head to lunch.

What do you guys have in your lunches?
I forgot mine, so I have to eat the cafeteria food.
Cafeteria food?! Those lunches are assembled by machines, you know!

I like our new cafeteria.
It's so futuristic!

Why isn't Mr. Bailey eating lunch?
Maybe he ate in the teachers' lounge.
Maybe he DOESN'T eat because he's a ROBOT!

Why are you kids always so spaced out after lunch?
This afternoon, I'm going to test—

TEST?! I knew it! Another test so you can assign numbers to all of us for when you become our ROBOT OVERLORD!

What? No, I was saying I'm going to test your writing skills.
I bet we aren't even allowed to use our imaginations!
Of course you can!

Really?
Yes! It's CREATIVE writing!
You can write whatever you want!

RINNGGGGG
See you tomorrow, Fred!

GGGGGGGGG!
01110100 01101000
01100101 01100101
01101110 01100100
00111111

How was school, Fred?

Boring.